Sleepover Squad

#2 Camping Out

Grab your pillow and join the

Sleepover Squad

P. J. DENTON

Sleepover Squad

#2 Camping Out

Illustrated by Julia Denos

ALADDIN PAPERBACKS

NEW YORK LONDON TORONTO SYDNEY

ALADDIN PAPERBACKS

An imprint of Simon & Schuster Children's Publishing Division

1230 Avenue of the Americas, New York, NY 10020

Text copyright © 2007 by Catherine Hapka

Illustrations copyright © 2007 by Julia Denos

All rights reserved, including the right of reproduction in whole or in part in any form.

ALADDIN PAPERBACKS and related logo are registered trademarks of Simon & Schuster, Inc.

Designed by Karin Paprocki

The text of this book was set in Cochin.

Manufactured in the United States of America

First Aladdin Paperbacks edition May 2007

4 6 8 10 9 7 5 3

Library of Congress Control Number 2006928972

ISBN-13: 978-1-4169-2791-4

ISBN-10: 1-4169-2791-3

Sleepover Squad

#2 Camping Out

✳ 1 ✳

A Summery Sleepover

"Okay, you guys," Taylor Kent said. "It's time to decide where we're going to have our next sleepover party."

Taylor and her three best friends were spending a sunny midsummer afternoon at the Maple Street Swim Club. They had just spent a couple of hours playing tetherball and Marco Polo. Now they were drying off by lying on their beach towels at the edge of the main pool.

Kara Wyatt groaned and reached up to

squeeze more water out of her thick, wavy red hair. "Do we have to decide now? It's too hot to talk!" she said.

"It's been hot all summer," Taylor teased. "And you still manage to do plenty of talking."

Jo Sanchez laughed. "Good one, Taylor."

Instead of answering them, Kara flopped over from her back to her stomach

and let out another loud groan. She liked to be dramatic that way.

Emily McDougal sat up and reached for her tube of sunscreen. Emily had very fair skin that burned easily. Her parents insisted that she reapply her sunscreen at least every couple of hours.

She squirted white goo out of the tube and started rubbing it on her arms. "I guess

we should talk about it soon," she said.

But she didn't sound very eager. Sitting out in the sun seemed to be making everyone except Taylor feel a little lazy. Taylor almost never felt lazy. Her mother liked to say that she had been born doing jumping jacks and that she hadn't slowed down since.

"We were supposed to have a sleepover every weekend, remember?" Taylor reminded her friends. "That's why we formed the Sleepover Squad. But it's been over a month since the first party at my house."

Emily stopped rubbing in sunscreen for a second and squinted at Taylor. "That's true," she said. "I didn't realize it had been that long."

"It *has* been a while." Jo sat up. She tilted her head to one side, the way she often did while solving problems at the board in math class, then said, "Thirty-three days, to be exact."

Taylor smiled. Jo always liked to be exact. "So what are we waiting for?" Taylor asked. She scraped her big toe across the scratchy pavement at the pool's edge. Then she dipped it into the cool water. "One of you needs to ask your parents if you can have the next party."

"Yeah." Kara yawned. "I would do it, but my older brothers just got home from baseball camp. And they don't leave for soccer camp for two weeks." She wrinkled her nose. "And, of course, my little brothers are home all summer."

Taylor smiled sympathetically at her friend. Kara was always complaining about having four rambunctious brothers. She made them sound like monsters, and it was true that they could be pests sometimes. Still, Taylor thought it might be kind of fun to have a bunch of other kids around all the time—even boys. It would be like having her own personal basketball team, right there in the same house.

"Okay, Kara's place is out," she said. "Emmers? What about you? You were talking about maybe having the next sleepover at your house, right?"

Emily nodded and pushed back a strand of her damp, pale blond hair. "I remember," she said, but she sounded distracted. She squirted out another dollop of sunscreen.

Taylor watched her. Emily had already put on sunscreen twice since they'd arrived at the pool. Taylor was glad she didn't have to worry that much about sunscreen—her African-American skin didn't burn as quickly as Emily's very pale skin did. "So did you ask your parents?" she asked Emily.

"Not yet, but I—Oh!" Suddenly, Emily sat up straight, looking excited. The sunscreen tube slipped out of her hand and bounced on the pavement. Jo caught it just before it rolled into the pool.

"What's wrong, Em?" Kara sat up and

stared at her. "Did a mosquito bite you? They've been biting me all day." She scratched at a pink bump on her freckled arm, then at another on her ankle.

Emily smiled. "No, not a mosquito," she said. "But a great idea just bit me!"

It took Taylor a second to figure out what her friend was saying. Sometimes Emily talked like someone from one of the books she was always reading. It could be a little confusing. Taylor always found it easier just to say what you meant straight out.

"You mean you have an idea?" Taylor asked. "Is it about our next slumber party?"

"Yes." Emily's blue eyes sparkled. "I just remembered something. My parents got a new tent last week. I could ask them if we can use it. That way, we could camp out in the backyard for our next sleepover!"

Jo gasped. "That would be so much fun!"

"Definitely!" Kara clapped her hands.

Her freckled cheeks were already pink from being out in the sun all day. But now they went even pinker with excitement. "What an amazing idea! It's the perfect summer sleepover plan!"

"I can ask my dad to cook hot dogs for us on the grill," Emily said. "And being outside in the dark will make our spooky stories even spookier!"

"My mom always talks about going camping," Jo said. "She used to camp out with her sisters and cousins all the time when she was our age. She likes to tell stories about catching fireflies and falling asleep to chirping crickets."

Taylor was glad the others were finally getting excited about the next sleepover. But she wasn't very excited about the camping idea herself. She stared out at the people splashing around in the pool, trying to figure out how to tell her friends that.

"Listen, guys," she said. "Camping could be fun. But it might be too hot to sleep outside."

Emily shrugged. "My house doesn't have air-conditioning," she said. "So we'll be hot either way if the party is at my house."

"Oh." Taylor hadn't thought of that. "Okay. But what if it rains?"

"It's not supposed to rain until next week," Jo said.

Taylor didn't bother to question her. Jo usually knew what she was talking about. "Okay," she said, trying to think of another argument. "But—"

"Hey, Em, do you have a croquet set?" Kara interrupted eagerly. "I've always wanted to learn to play croquet. But our yard isn't big enough. Plus, my brothers would probably just beat one another over the head with the mallets."

Jo giggled. "That sounds like your brothers."

"We have a croquet set," Emily said with a smile. "I'll teach you how to play, Kara."

"Can we fly kites?" Jo asked. "My mom talks about doing that a lot too."

"That sounds like fun," Emily agreed. "When I ask my parents about the campout and the croquet set, I'll ask them if we can get the kites out of the attic."

Taylor opened her mouth to argue against the campout idea. But then she closed it again. She could tell it was no use. Everyone in the Sleepover Squad was excited about their plan of sleeping outside in a tent. Everyone except her.

She bit her lip, not sure what she was going to do. How could she admit the *real* reason she didn't want to camp out?

✳ 2 ✳

Taylor's Secret

Just then Jo looked at her watch. It was waterproof, so she could wear it even at the pool. "Hey, Taylor," she said. "You told me to tell you when it's almost two fifteen. It's ten minutes after two right now."

"Thanks." Taylor jumped to her feet and picked up her towel. "I've got to go. I have soccer practice today."

Kara looked disappointed. "But we just started planning our campout sleepover!" she complained.

"That's okay. You guys can keep planning without me." Taylor smiled, trying to seem normal. She didn't want her friends to guess her secret. Not until she figured out the best way to tell them. And right now she didn't have time—she didn't want to be late for soccer practice.

She said good-bye, grabbed her pool bag, and headed toward the exit. There was no running allowed in the pool area, so Taylor just walked as quickly as she could. The hot cement burned her feet, but she didn't put on her flip-flops until she reached the big metal gates at the entrance. Then she paused long enough to slip them on.

She spotted a familiar bright blue car as soon as she stepped through the gates. The car belonged to the Kents' housekeeper, Gloria. Both of Taylor's parents had busy jobs, so Gloria was the one who drove Taylor around during the day. Luckily, Taylor could walk to the swim club from her house, so Gloria didn't have to drive her there. Taylor was also allowed to walk to Kara's house or to the ice-cream parlor as long as she told Gloria where she was going and called when she got there. But her soccer league met on a field at the high school, which was a couple of miles away at the edge of town.

Taylor stepped out onto the gravel parking lot. She had to walk carefully so no gravel would get between her toes.

"Put your towel on the seat," Gloria said when Taylor opened the car's back door. "You're soaking wet."

Taylor didn't think that was true. In fact, her hair and bathing suit were almost dry. But she did as Gloria said and spread her towel on the backseat before she got in. It was always easier to do as Gloria said.

Gloria started the car. Then she looked at Taylor in the rearview mirror. "You all right, *chica*?" she asked. "You look a little down."

Taylor usually made a joke when Gloria called her *chica*. She knew that *chica* was just a Spanish word for "girl." But she always pretended she thought Gloria was calling her a chicken.

Today, however, Taylor wasn't in a joking mood. She hated keeping secrets from her friends. Now, suddenly, she found herself with a big one. And it definitely wasn't the kind that would be easy to share.

"I'm okay," she said. "Hey, Gloria, I was just wondering something. Are you afraid of anything?"

Gloria stopped the car at a stop sign. Then she glanced back at Taylor again. "Me, afraid?" she said. "Why do you ask?"

"No reason," Taylor said quickly. She wasn't ready to tell anyone what was worrying her. "I was just curious."

She already felt a little bit silly for asking. Gloria wasn't the type of person to be afraid of anything. She was always telling stories about all the crazy things she and her brother had done while growing up in Puerto Rico.

"Oh." Gloria shrugged. "Well, if you must know, I do have a terrible fear of heights. Once my brother convinced me to climb a very tall tree. When I reached the top branches, I was too terrified to climb down again. Our papa had to come out and rescue me." She laughed. "He teases me about it to this day!"

"Really?" Taylor grinned. It was funny to imagine Gloria, with her carefully pressed clothes and neat black and gray bun, clinging to the branches of a tree. "So you were really afraid?"

"I was really afraid," Gloria said. "I also don't like looking out windows in tall buildings or driving over large bridges. I know it's silly, but those things always make me feel dizzy and anxious."

"Wow." Somehow, hearing that even someone as sensible as Gloria had silly fears made Taylor feel a tiny bit better about her own secret.

"I'll tell you something else that frightens me," Gloria said. "It's that you won't have your soccer clothes on by the time we get to the field."

"Oops!" Taylor realized they were almost there. She grabbed the bag of clothes on the car floor and pulled on her shorts and T-shirt over her swimsuit. She was still lacing up her cleats when Gloria turned the car into the high school parking lot.

The playing fields were swarming with kids. At least three summer league teams, including Taylor's, were practicing that day. When she got out of the car, she looked for the bright green T-shirts that matched the one she was wearing. The shirts said MCDOUGAL ORGANIC WARRIORS on them. Taylor's team was named after Emily's mother's plant and vegetable business, McDougal Organic Nursery. The nursery was the team's sponsor, which meant Mrs. McDougal helped pay for the uniforms and equipment.

Taylor said good-bye to Gloria. Then she jogged across the fields toward the other kids in green shirts. Several of her teammates saw her coming and waved or shouted out her name.

"Yo, Kent!" a boy named Curtis Cohen called. "It's about time you showed up."

"Zip your lip, Cohen," Taylor yelled back with a grin. "No matter what time I show up, I still play better than you!"

Another teammate, Essie Anderson, laughed and gave Taylor a high five. "You tell him, Taylor," she said. "Curtis couldn't score a goal even if the net was ten miles wide."

Taylor giggled. She knew Essie was just kidding around. Curtis was one of the best players on their team. In their last game he'd scored more goals than anyone except Taylor.

Curtis ran over and gave Essie a playful shove. "Oh yeah?" he said. "The only thing around here that's ten miles wide is your mouth!"

Just then the assistant coach, a college student named Chloe, walked toward them. "Get stretching, people," she called out. "We'll be starting in a few minutes."

Taylor dropped to the grass and started

doing the stretching exercises the coaches had taught them. Essie sat down beside her.

"Were you at the pool today?" Essie asked between stretches. "I can see your bathing suit straps under your shirt."

"Yeah, I just came from there," Taylor said as she leaned forward to touch her toes. "My friends and I were . . ."

She forgot what she was saying mid-sentence as she felt somebody grab the back of her shirt. A second later something small and wriggly tickled her back.

"Hey!" Essie cried. "Very funny, Curtis!"

"Check it out!" a boy standing nearby shouted gleefully. "Curtis put a spider down Taylor's back!"

"Ooh, watch out, Curtis!" another teammate cried. "She's going to pound you for that one."

"She'll probably stick that spider up his nose!" someone called out with a laugh.

But Taylor hardly heard what any of them were saying. She leaped to her feet, shaking her arms and yelling. "Get it off me!" she shrieked. "Get it off me!"

She could feel the spider wriggling down her back. The sensation made her feel panicky. She jumped up and down and spun around in circles. The more she moved, the more she seemed to feel the

spider's hairy little legs scrabbling around on her skin. It felt as if there were spiders crawling all over her!

"Chill out, Taylor," Essie said. "It's just a spider. Hold still and I'll—"

"Don't tell me to chill out!" Taylor yelled. *"Just get it off!"*

Chloe hurried over. "Hold still," she ordered sharply.

The assistant coach's voice stopped Taylor's jumping for a second. Chloe grabbed Taylor by the shoulder, spun her around, and tugged at the back of her shirt.

"There it is!" Essie cried, pointing. "It just fell out."

Taylor leaped forward. Then she glanced back over her shoulder and saw a small black creature scurrying off through the grass. Her whole body went limp with relief.

She looked around and found almost the

whole team gathered around. Her team-mates were all staring at her in surprise.

"Yo, check it out, guys," Curtis said, his eyes wide with amazement. "Tough Taylor Kent is afraid of bugs!"

✳ 3 ✳

Never Surrender!

Taylor didn't embarrass easily. But she was embarrassed now. She couldn't believe the whole soccer field had just heard her terrible secret. It was true: Ever since she could remember, she'd been scared of having spiders or other creepy-crawly types of bugs touch her. Most people never would have guessed it. After all, Taylor loved playing sports and being outdoors. But even the idea of tiny little legs crawling on her gave her the creeps.

"Shut up, Curtis," she muttered, hanging her head and staring at her own feet. "You're so immature."

Chloe clapped her hands. "All right, people," she said. "I see Coach Summers heading this way. Let's take your places. . . ." She started calling out which positions she wanted everyone to take.

Taylor was glad. She wanted to stop thinking about what had just happened. She jogged toward her position as soon as Chloe called her name.

Essie quickly fell into step beside her. "Don't worry, Taylor," she said. "It's no big deal if you don't like spiders. I freak out if I even *see* a snake. And my uncle is afraid of mice."

"Yeah, okay." Taylor didn't feel like talking about it anymore. "We'd better get in position now."

A moment later the coach arrived and practice started. Curtis made spider fingers at Taylor the first few times he passed close to her. But nobody else said anything about what had happened. By the time they started doing shooting drills, even Curtis seemed to forget all about it.

Still, Taylor couldn't stop thinking about it. She missed two easy shots in a row because she was so distracted.

"Focus, Kent!" the coach barked at her.

"Sorry," Taylor called out.

She was annoyed with herself. It was bad enough to be afraid of something so dumb. But it was even worse to let it ruin her game.

As she walked back to the end of the line, she realized there was one good thing about what had happened. Now there was no reason not to tell her friends why she didn't want to camp out. She might as well admit she was terrified at the thought of sleeping on the ground, where all kinds of spiders and other bugs could crawl on her. Now that her entire soccer team knew, the news would be all over town before long.

Taylor made a face. How could a thought like that make her feel better and worse at the same time?

As soon as she got home, Taylor headed for the phone in the front sitting room. Gloria was busy in the kitchen at the back of the house, and neither of Taylor's parents was home from work yet. That was good. Taylor didn't want anything to interrupt her. Once she made up her mind to do something, she liked to do it right away.

She dialed Emily's number first. Someone answered on the second ring.

"Good afternoon," a crisp voice said. "McDougal Organic Nursery. How may I help you?"

"Hi, Mrs. M," Taylor said, recognizing

Emily's mother's voice. "This is Taylor. Is Emily there?"

"Hi, Taylor. I'm sorry, she's not home right now. She and her father just left for the grocery store to get supplies for your party."

Taylor was surprised. "She asked you about the sleepover already?" she asked.

Mrs. McDougal chuckled. "Yes," she said. "She was so excited, she couldn't wait. It's going to be tomorrow night—if you can make it then?"

Taylor thought about saying she couldn't come the next night. But she didn't think about it for long. She hated lying.

"Yes," she said instead. "I think I can make it then. I just need to check with my parents to be sure."

She said good-bye and hung up. Then she stared at the phone and chewed on her lower lip. Was it already too late to change her friends' minds?

"No way," she whispered to herself. "All I have to do is explain why we need to move the party inside. . . ."

She picked up the phone again. This time she dialed Kara's number. All she got was a busy signal. She hung up and tried again. Same thing.

"Rats," she said. "Stupid brothers."

Kara's house had only one phone line. Her brothers were always tying it up by spending hours playing goofy computer games online. They always got in trouble when Kara's parents caught them. But they always ended up doing it again.

With a sigh, Kara punched in Jo's number. Jo was the most sensible of them all, anyway. If Taylor could make her understand, Jo could help her explain it to the others.

Jo's mother answered the phone. "Oh, hello, honey," Mrs. Sanchez said when she heard it was Taylor. "Jo just got picked up for her tennis lesson. Is this about your campout tomorrow night? Jo's so excited about it, and no wonder! Some of my favorite memories involve camping out. . . . But never mind. Shall I have her call you when she gets home?"

"Um, no, that's okay," Taylor said. "It's nothing important. Thanks anyway."

After Taylor hung up, she flopped onto the antique sofa in front of the fireplace. She wasn't usually the type of person who wasted a lot of time sitting around worrying. But today she couldn't help it. Her friends were all superexcited about the campout idea. How could Taylor ruin their fun just because she was a wimp when it came to bugs?

Just then the front door swung open. "Hello, hello! Anybody home?" Taylor's father cried, striding in with his suit jacket slung over one shoulder.

"Dad?" Taylor sat up, surprised.

Normally, her father didn't arrive home from his law office until just before dinnertime. "What are you doing home so early?"

Mr. Kent turned and spotted her. He had a big grin on his face as he walked into the sitting room.

"I decided to give myself the rest of the afternoon off," he said. He dropped his jacket on the arm of the sofa and reached over to give Taylor's head a rub. "I'm celebrating—I just won that big case I've been working on all summer."

"Really? That's cool." Despite her worries, Taylor smiled. It was nice to see her dad in such a cheerful mood.

"It's more than cool." Her father grinned. "Everyone and their brother expected me to lose this case, and lose big. But I guess I showed them!" He winked. "Just goes to prove my motto: Never surrender!"

Taylor giggled. Her father's good mood was catching. She already felt a little bit

better than she had a few minutes ago.
"Never surrender!" she said, pumping her
fist. "Congratulations, Dad."

Her father hurried off toward the kitchen
to share his news with Gloria. Taylor stayed
where she was. She was thinking about
what he had just said.

Maybe she was looking at this campout situation all wrong. Maybe her dad's motto could work for her problem, too. Why should Taylor give in to her own fears? Why should she let the thought of a few creepy crawlies spoil everybody's fun, including her own?

Suddenly, she was glad she hadn't reached any of her friends on the phone. Because she had just decided *not* to tell them about her fear . . . at least not until *after* the campout the next night. That way, by the time she told them the truth, it wouldn't matter anymore. By then she would have overcome her silly fear.

"Never surrender!" she whispered to herself.

* 4 *

The Big Day

Taylor had a nervous knot in her stomach when she woke up the next morning. For a second she couldn't remember why. She lay there sleepily, staring up at her ceiling. Did she have a big game today? Was it already the first day of school? Or . . .

Suddenly, she remembered: Today was the day of the campout. That made Taylor wake up in a hurry.

"Never surrender," she whispered to

herself again. Then she sat up and swung her feet over the edge of her bed.

If she was going to do this, she was going to do it full speed ahead. That was just the way she was. So for the next few hours she barely stopped moving. She did everything she could think of to get ready for the sleepover. She took everything out of her dresser drawers and closets so she could decide which clothes and pajamas to pack. She vacuumed the inside and outside of her suitcase. She packed and unpacked her things twice. She wrote down ideas for games and activities for that night. She called her friends to see how their preparations were going.

"I'm glad you're so excited about the campout," Emily said when Taylor called her for the third time. "At first I wasn't sure you were."

Taylor didn't know what to say to that. Luckily, Emily's mother called her just then, and she had to get off the phone.

Finally, it was time to leave for Emily's house. Kara's mother had offered to pick up Taylor and Jo and drive them to the party. Taylor waited for her outside on the front porch with her suitcase, sleeping bag, and pillow. She spotted the Wyatts' minivan as soon as it turned onto her street.

Kara was riding in the seat right behind her mother. She waved through the open window. Taylor grabbed her stuff and jogged down the front walk.

"Sorry, Taylor!" Kara called. "We're stuck riding with the bratty boys. They insisted on coming along."

"Kara!" Mrs. Wyatt warned. "Don't talk about your brothers that way."

Kara rolled her eyes when her mother wasn't looking. Taylor grinned and slid open the van's back door.

"Hi there, Carrottop Twins," she said.

That was what she always called Mark and Todd Wyatt. They were six years old and looked almost exactly alike, from their tousled red hair to their scuffed sneakers. The only way to tell them apart was by the pattern of freckles on their faces.

"Hi, Taylor," Todd said as Taylor took a seat next to Kara, right in front of the two boys. "We decided to come to your sleepover too."

"Fat chance!" Kara cried, turning around to glare at them.

Mrs. Wyatt glanced at the kids over her shoulder. "Don't tease your sister, boys," she said with a smile. "You know this slumber party is for girls only."

"Girls stink!" Mark said, sticking out his tongue at Kara.

"Boys stink worse!" Kara replied.

Mrs. Wyatt sighed. "Can't you kids *try* to get along for at least ten minutes?"

But Kara and her brothers argued the

rest of the way to Jo's house. The Sanchez family lived in a nice subdivision at the edge of town. Their house was on a cul-de-sac with four other houses. When Mrs. Wyatt drove in, Jo was standing in her front yard watching her teenage neighbors play basketball.

Soon she was squeezed in beside Taylor in the backseat while Kara apologized for her brothers' presence. "It's okay," Jo said with a grin. "Actually, it's lucky there's no more room in the van. Otherwise, I think my mother would have invited herself along to the campout. She's even more excited about it than I am!"

Mrs. Wyatt smiled at Jo in the rearview mirror. "Does your mother enjoy camping?" she asked. "That's nice. I wouldn't have guessed that about her."

It gave Taylor a weird feeling whenever she remembered that all their parents didn't know one another that well. How could that be the case, when the four of them were such good friends?

But she didn't think about that for long. It took less than ten minutes to drive from Jo's house to Emily's. That meant it wouldn't be long until the camp-out started. In just a few hours they

would all be sleeping in a tent outside. Or *trying* to sleep, in Taylor's case.

Never surrender, she reminded herself silently.

When they reached Emily's house, Mr. McDougal came out with Emily to help the other girls unload their things from the back of the van. Taylor stacked her sleeping bag on top of her suitcase on the front lawn.

"Well, hello, fellows," Mr. McDougal said cheerfully as Kara's brothers hopped out of the van. "I didn't realize you two were in there."

Kara spun around and scowled at the twins. "Get back in the car!" she said. "You're not supposed to get out."

"It's okay, Kara," Emily said. She sounded a little bit worried. Emily didn't like it when people fought. She always tried to smooth things over if she could. "We don't mind if they run around for a few minutes. Right, Daddy?"

"Right." Mr. McDougal ruffled Todd's hair as the little boy darted past him. "There's plenty of room to run here."

That was true. Emily's yard was bigger than Taylor's, Kara's, and Jo's put together. There was a wide front lawn and an enormous vegetable garden off to the right side of the house. That was all Taylor could see from the driveway. But she had been there often enough to know that there was a fruit orchard behind the garden. Next to that was a large, grassy backyard. It was almost as big as the sports fields at the high school. A forest came right up to the yard on two sides, and on the far side of the orchard was a neighboring farmer's hay field.

"Thanks, Arthur," Mrs. Wyatt said gratefully to Emily's father. "It would be nice for them to get some energy out."

"Maybe they'll run away and never come back," Kara said, sounding grumpy.

She scowled as she watched the boys run around.

Taylor made a scary monster face as Mark ran toward her. "Aaargh!" she growled playfully.

Both twins screamed and raced off in the other direction. Taylor laughed. No matter what Kara said, her brothers could be fun sometimes.

"Come on," Emily said to her friends. "We can come get your stuff in a little while. I want to show you the tent!"

"Cool!" Jo said eagerly.

"I'll be right there," Taylor said. "First I need to catch the twins and throw them in the creek. Aaargh!" She chased after the boys for a few steps. They screeched with laughter and kept running across the yard.

Meanwhile, Emily headed for the front door. "Hey," Kara called, sounding surprised. "Where are you going, Em? Did you set up the tent inside the house?"

Mr. McDougal was still chatting with Mrs. Wyatt. But he looked over when he heard Kara's comment.

"We didn't set up the tent yet," he told her. "If you girls are going to sleep in it, you also have to help me set it up."

"Cool!" Jo said again. "That sounds like fun."

Taylor gulped and turned away from the twins. Every time someone mentioned the tent, she got more nervous.

She followed her friends inside. Emily's house was even older than hers. It had creaky wooden floors, two staircases, and lots of interesting nooks and crannies. There were plants everywhere. Pictures of plants hung on the walls. Books about plants loaded the bookshelves in every room. Real plants in colorful pots sat on all the windowsills.

The girls hurried through the kitchen

and out to the mudroom. That was a sunny room at the back of the house between the kitchen and the back porch. It contained the washer and dryer, a wall of hooks for hanging up coats, and food and water dishes for Emily's cat, Mi-Mo.

The tent was lying in the middle of the floor. At least Taylor guessed it was the tent. It looked more like a big, messy pile of dark blue canvas and metal poles.

"Is that it?" Kara wrinkled her nose. She didn't look impressed.

Emily nodded. "Don't worry, it looks a lot better when it's up. We can start putting it together as soon as Daddy gets here. First we'll need to screw together these poles, and . . . oops!"

She dropped the pole she was holding. Then she giggled.

"What?" Jo asked.

Emily pointed. "That spider startled me," she said. "When I picked up the pole,

it started to crawl onto my hand."

Taylor shuddered. The campout hadn't even started yet, and the first spider had already appeared!

She watched while Emily grabbed a baseball cap hanging on one of the coat hooks. Using the hat's stiff brim, she carefully picked up the spider and carried it to the back door. Jo opened the door for her, and Emily gently dumped the spider outside.

Taylor shuddered again as the door closed. Normally, it wouldn't bother her to *see* a spider as long as it didn't *touch* her. But today was different. Today all she could think about was that in a few hours she would be sleeping outside, where lots of spiders might crawl on her. The thought made her skin crawl.

Could she really do this?

✳ 5 ✳

Fun and Games

The others didn't notice Taylor's reaction. Emily's parents had just walked into the mudroom.

"Ready to get started on the tent, girls?" Mr. McDougal asked. "I hope we got all the pieces out of the attic. Otherwise, you might have to take turns staying awake to hold up the roof!"

Kara and Emily giggled. Jo looked doubtful.

"I don't think that would work," Jo said.

"All the poles probably have to be connected together. If even one is missing, it couldn't stand up at all. Not even with someone holding it."

That made Taylor laugh a little. "Don't worry, Jojo," she said. "I think Mr. M was only kidding around."

"Oh." Jo looked slightly sheepish. "Yeah, I knew that."

Mrs. McDougal grabbed the stack of poles. "I've got these," she said. "You four can help Emily's dad carry the fabric outside."

Taylor hung back as her friends crowded forward to grab the edges of the canvas. The skin on the back of her hands felt itchy as she thought about that spider. What if the spider had a friend still hiding in the folds of the tent? What if there was a whole nest of baby spiders in there, just waiting to swarm out over her arms?

"Can you get that corner, Taylor?" Emily said.

Taylor blinked and stepped forward. "Um . . . okay." She grabbed the fabric, but she used only the ends of her fingers to hold it.

Mrs. McDougal had already dropped the poles outside. She returned to hold open the back door. It was hard for the others to walk together and carry the tent through the narrow opening. But Jo started calling out "left, right, left, right," and soon they had the tent out in the backyard.

Taylor dropped her corner as soon as she could. She backed away and looked down at her hands. No spiders.

She felt kind of stupid for being so nervous. She wasn't supposed to be scared of anything! But she couldn't seem to stop thinking about bugs and spiders.

The others were already sorting out the poles and screwing them together. Taylor walked around and poked at tent parts with the toe of her sneaker. She was trying to look like she was helping without having to touch the tent very much.

Luckily, the others were having too much fun to notice. Taylor was relieved. Maybe she could pull this off after all!

Before long the tent was up. It had a pointy top and a zippered flap for a door. Thick ropes held down the corners to keep it from blowing in the breeze. They had set it up in a nice, open spot on one side of the back lawn, halfway between the wooden picnic table and the edge of the woods. When they were all quiet, they could hear the burble and splash of the little stream that tumbled along a few yards inside the tree line.

"This is awesome!" Jo said, her brown eyes shining as she looked around.

Kara nodded, clapping her hands. "Let's go check out the inside now," she said.

"We can tell stories or something."

"Have fun, girls," Mr. McDougal said. "Let me know when you get hungry, and I'll fire up the grill."

"Thanks, Daddy," Emily said.

As Mr. and Mrs. McDougal walked away, Emily, Kara, and Jo crowded through the door flap. Taylor took a deep breath and followed them. She had to duck her head to fit through.

Inside the tent it was dim and shadowy. The thick, dark-colored canvas kept out most of the sun's light.

"Shouldn't we bring some flashlights or something?" Taylor asked. Her eyes darted around to the dark corners. Were there creepy crawlies hiding back there? It would be awfully easy for spiders or other bugs to crawl in through the openings in the canvas. . . .

"We'll get some lanterns from the house later," Emily said. She sat down cross-legged on the canvas floor. "It's light enough for now, though."

Taylor wasn't so sure. She wasn't afraid of the dark. But being inside the dimly lit tent was making her nervous. She watched as Jo and Kara sat down too.

"Hey!" she said, backing toward the flap. "Are you guys nuts? We shouldn't waste a perfect summer day inside—even if it's inside a tent! I thought we were going to play croquet and fly kites and stuff. And I brought a soccer ball in case we want to play keep-away or something."

"But sitting in here is fun too," Kara said. "Maybe we should hang out for a while."

"No way." Taylor shook her head. "We have all night to sit around in here."

Emily giggled. "You guys should know by now that it's impossible to get Taylor to sit still," she told Kara and Jo.

Taylor was glad nobody had guessed the real reason she wanted to leave the tent. "That's right," she said. "If you don't come outside, I'll go get my soccer ball and start kicking it around in here."

Jo stood up. "Come on, you guys," she said. "I think she means it." She led the way out of the tent.

Once she was out in the fresh air, Taylor immediately felt much better. As long as she was busy running around and doing things, she wouldn't have time to think about scary bugs.

"So what do you want to do first?" she asked the others. She was in the mood for soccer, as usual. But she didn't say so. Now that they were outside, she didn't really care what they did.

"Croquet," Kara said. "Em, you promised to teach me to play."

Emily went to get the croquet set, and the girls played for a while. Emily taught Kara the rules, but Kara wasn't very good. She kept hitting her own foot with her mallet. Then she would say "ow" and start giggling. Taylor and Emily both played a little better than Kara, but Jo won the first three games in a row.

"Maybe all my tennis lessons helped make me good at croquet, too," Jo said. "And I didn't even know it!"

Taylor grinned. "I guess so," she said. "I'll have to practice more if I want to win next time." Taylor was the best of all her friends at sports. Usually the only thing Jo could beat her at was tennis. Now she would have to add croquet to the list.

After one more game of croquet—Jo won again—they switched to Freeze Tag. By the time the last person was "frozen" for the third time, everyone was getting hungry and thirsty.

Kara collapsed to the ground. "I'm dying of thirst," she moaned. "I can't play anymore."

"Okay, let's go inside," Emily said. "Mom squeezed a whole pitcher of lemonade earlier."

Taylor licked her lips. Mrs. McDougal's homemade lemonade was delicious. "Let's go!" she said.

Soon they were back outside, each of them holding a tall, icy glass of lemonade. They carried them over to the picnic table. Taylor checked the wooden seat carefully before she sat down. No spiders.

Mr. McDougal came outside and hurried over to the grill, which was nearby. He lifted the cover.

"I'll get this started," he told them. "The hot dogs should be ready in fifteen or twenty minutes."

"Great." Kara patted her stomach. "After all that running around, I'm starved!"

Emily giggled. "You're always starved," she teased.

"That's true. But right now *I'm* starved too," Jo said. "My mom always says camping made her hungrier than just about anything else."

"It's more fun than just about anything else too!" Kara said. "Hey, maybe *all* our summer sleepovers should be campouts from now on."

Taylor's heart sank when she heard that. But she didn't say anything.

In fact, she didn't say anything for the next ten minutes. She sat there sipping her lemonade and sneaking looks at the tent standing nearby. How many spiders were crawling around in there right that minute?

Finally, Jo noticed how quiet she was being. "Earth to Taylor," she joked. "What's got you distracted now?"

The others also turned to look at her. Taylor thought about just telling them all the truth. As her mother liked to say, that was always the easiest answer.

Then she thought about what her father liked to say: Never surrender. That made her wonder if admitting her fear to her friends might be like giving up. She knew her friends would offer to move the sleepover inside if she told them what was bothering her. But how could she overcome her fear if she didn't face it?

"Nothing," she said, deciding to stick with her plan. She would tell them the truth in the morning—not before. "Except that I'm starving to death!" She turned in her seat to look at Emily's father, who was poking at the hot dogs sizzling on the grill. "Hey, Mr. M, when are those dogs going to be hot?"

✳ 6 ✳

Wasting Time

By the time the girls finished eating their dinner of grilled hot dogs, lemonade, and a delicious salad of fresh greens picked from Mrs. McDougal's garden, the sun was starting to go down. Kara sat back and burped.

"Excuse me," she said with a chuckle.

"There's no excuse for you," Taylor joked. Even though she was worried about her problem, it was still fun being with her friends.

"Come on, let's take our dishes inside," Emily said, standing up. "Then we can change into our pajamas and come back out."

The girls gathered up their paper plates, napkins, and forks. When they got inside, they found that Mr. and Mrs. McDougal had brought their suitcases and sleeping bags into the mudroom.

"Grab your pajamas. We can change up in my room," Emily suggested.

Taylor loved Emily's room. It was filled with books, toy horses, and pretty hand-made quilts and rugs, which made it the perfect room for Emily. Her cat, Mi-Mo, was sleeping on the bed. When the girls came in, he woke up and sat up. Then he started washing his foot with his pink tongue.

While the others started changing, Taylor wandered around, looking at the titles of the books on the bookshelves. But she wasn't really paying attention to the books. Instead, she was thinking good thoughts to try to pump herself up for the sleepover. It was the same thing she did before every big soccer game. Before a soccer game she usually thought things like *I can help my team win this game* and *Go for the goal.* This time she was thinking, *Camping out is great* and *Spiders are no big deal.* Her good thoughts almost always worked before a soccer game. But they weren't working too well tonight. She still felt nervous.

Kara looked up from pulling on her pink nightie. "Hurry up, Taylor," she said. "We want to get back out there."

"Yeah," Jo said, holding up her toothbrush. "And we still have to brush our teeth."

Taylor realized the others were all changed already. "Okay," she said. "You guys can go ahead to the bathroom if you want. I'll be right there."

The others hurried out of the room, talking about how they should arrange their sleeping bags in the tent. Taylor watched them go. Then she picked up her favorite frog-print pajamas, which she'd dropped on Emily's bed. Mi-Mo stopped licking his foot and watched her.

"I'm just being silly, aren't I, Mi-Mo?" Taylor said to the cat. "Bugs and spiders are nothing to be afraid of. I probably stomp on dozens of them by accident every time I play soccer."

Mi-Mo answered by licking his paw again. Taylor sighed. The later it got, the more she worried about spiders crawling on her while she slept. She was annoyed with herself for being so scared. But she couldn't seem to do anything about it.

She changed into her pajamas as slowly as she could. As she was putting on her slippers, Emily returned.

"Are you ready yet?" she asked. "I left the toothpaste cap off for you."

"Thanks." Taylor smiled at her friend.

Once again, she was tempted to tell the truth. If anyone would understand, Emily would. After all, she was afraid of all sorts of things—big dogs, speaking in front of the class, crossing busy streets, and more. And she didn't seem to mind if other people knew it.

But Taylor wasn't like that. She hated

being afraid. That was why she was determined to get over her fear of bugs.

Kara appeared behind Emily in the doorway. "Hurry up!" she cried impatiently. "It's time to get this campout started for real!"

"Okay, okay," Taylor said. "Just let me brush my teeth and I'll be ready. I'll meet you guys downstairs."

"No way," Kara said. "You're too distractible. If we leave you in the bathroom by yourself, you'll probably forget what you're doing and start taking a bubble bath or something."

Taylor's friends were always teasing her about being distractible. Taylor didn't mind; she *was* distractible. There were always so many different interesting things to look at, do, or think about that it was impossible to focus on just one.

But tonight was different. Tonight Taylor was focused on only one thing: surviving the campout.

All three of her friends waited in the bath-room doorway while Taylor brushed her teeth. Then they dragged her downstairs. Mrs. McDougal was transplanting tiny plant seedlings at the kitchen table while Mr. McDougal washed dishes nearby. The tiny, old-fashioned black-and-white TV set on the counter was tuned to the local PBS station.

Seeing the TV gave Taylor a sudden idea. "Oh, I love this show," she said. "Maybe we should stay inside and watch it for a while."

Mrs. McDougal turned and stared at her in surprise. "You love this show?" she said. "I had no idea you were an opera fan, Taylor."

"She's not, Mommy," Emily said with a laugh. "She's just kidding around. Right, Taylor?"

"Um, right." Taylor looked around the kitchen for some other ideas. "Hey, you guys—remember how much fun it was decorating those cupcakes at our last party? Maybe we should do that again tonight. We could help Mr. M bake the cupcakes, and then—"

Kara didn't let her finish. "Forget it. This is a campout party, not a cupcake-making party!" She grabbed Taylor's arm and dragged her through the kitchen and into the mudroom.

When they got there, Taylor spied Mi-Mo's food dish. "Uh-oh, Emmers," she said. "Looks like your kitty is almost out of food." She pointed to the dish. "Maybe we'd better help you feed him."

Emily looked at the dish. "It's almost half full," she said. "I usually only have to fill it in the morning. Don't worry, he'll be fine."

Kara was still holding on to Taylor's left arm. Now Jo grabbed the right one, laughing.

"Come on, Miss Distractible," she said.
"We're supposed to be having a campout,
remember? Camp*out*. That means we need
to go *out*side."

Taylor couldn't think of any other ways
to delay. So she picked up her sleeping bag

and pillow and went out the back door with the others.

It was almost dark by now. Stars were twinkling in the sky overhead, and a slight breeze cooled the warm summer air. Crickets were already starting to chirp, along with the little tree frogs that lived near the stream in the woods.

Kara stopped and took a deep breath. "Aah, this is more like it," she said happily. "I can't wait to get this campout started!"

Emily had grabbed a pair of battery-powered lanterns from the mudroom. She turned them on and led the way into the tent. The lanterns made the inside almost as bright as a room in the house.

Taylor joined in with the others to unroll sleeping bags and fluff pillows. She was getting more and more nervous, though she did her best to hide it. How was she ever going to fall asleep out here?

Then she had an idea. It was much

better than the opera-watching idea or the cat-feeding idea. In fact, it was so simple and so brilliant that she couldn't believe she hadn't thought of it before.

She wasn't really afraid of bugs when she was awake—well, not unless obnoxious Curtis Cohen put one down her shirt, anyway. And she was pretty sure none of her best friends would ever do something like that.

So there was just one solution. She wouldn't go to sleep tonight!

Right away she felt much better about the whole campout. She turned and grinned at her friends. Kara was sitting cross-legged on her sleeping bag. Emily was adjusting one of the lanterns. Jo was flicking a stray leaf off her pillow.

"Okay, guys," Taylor said brightly, clapping her hands. "It's time to have some fun at this party!"

✴ 7 ✴

Staying Awake

"Okay," Emily said to Taylor. "What do you want to do first?"

Taylor thought for a second. What would help keep them all awake? "I know," she said. "Flashlight Tag!"

"Flashlight Tag?" Kara sounded dubious. "What's that?"

"It's sort of like Freeze Tag," Taylor explained. "Only instead of touching someone to freeze them, you need to catch them with your flashlight beam. It's the perfect game to play in the dark!"

Emily looked nervous as she glanced at the tent doorway. "That sounds a little scary."

"Yeah," Kara said. "It figures Taylor would come up with it. She probably thinks the rest of us will be so scared of the dark that she's sure to win!"

"Very funny," Taylor said as the others laughed. "Now come on. Are we playing or what?"

"I guess we could try it for a while," Jo said. "We all brought flashlights, right?"

Soon they were all outside playing Flashlight Tag. Taylor volunteered to be "it." Each of the other girls turned off her flashlight and sneaked off into the dark.

Taylor closed her eyes and counted to fifty to give them time to scatter. Then she opened her eyes. "Ready or not, here I come!" she called. She switched off her flashlight too.

Then she stood still for a minute, just listening. It felt kind of strange being outside in her pajamas. But it was also kind of fun.

There was some light coming from the house. Everywhere else in the yard was pitch-black. Being out in Emily's yard was much different from being in town, where there was always light from the streetlamps and from cars driving by. It was even darker than Jo's neighborhood, where there was usually plenty of light from the neighboring houses.

Taylor's heart beat a little faster, and she smiled. This was fun!

She heard a rustling sound nearby. It was coming from the direction of the woods. *Aha!* Taylor thought.

She tiptoed toward the sound. She had to move slowly so she wouldn't trip over a rock or a dip in the ground. When she thought she was close enough, she stopped and listened. The rustle came again.

Taylor lifted her flashlight and aimed it. Then she hit the button to turn it on.

"Gotcha!" she cried. Kara was standing there in the beam of light, looking wide-eyed and startled.

"Rats!" Kara said, flicking on her own flashlight. "I wanted to go farther away. But I was afraid I'd wander into the woods and get lost." She shuddered. "Plus, what if there are bears or something in there?"

Taylor rolled her eyes. "There are no bears around here," she said.

"Are you sure?" Kara glanced over her shoulder at the dark trees. Then she wrapped her arms around herself and shuddered. "There could be bears."

"You can ask Jo if you don't believe me," Taylor said with a smile. "Now come on—since I caught you, you get to help me find the others. Then you're it next time."

They kept playing for a while. When it was her turn to hide, Taylor hurried all the way to the orchard. She picked the oldest apple tree there and hid behind its thick, gnarled trunk. The others would never catch her there!

She was still hiding behind the tree when she heard a shriek. It came from closer to the house. She peered out from behind the tree trunk and saw that all three of her friends had their flashlights on.

A few seconds later she heard her friends calling her name. She turned on her own flashlight and jogged toward them.

"What's up?" she called. "Did I win that round?"

"Never mind that." Emily gestured toward Jo, who was sitting on the ground. "Jo hurt herself."

"I'm okay." Jo had one flip-flop off. She

was holding up her toe, staring at it with her flashlight. "I just stubbed my toe, that's all. I guess I tripped on something."

Emily looked worried. "I think it's too dark to play outside any longer," she said. "We'd better go back in the tent."

Taylor's heart sank. She wanted to convince her friends to stay outside. But she didn't want them getting hurt.

Emily was the first one to reach the tent. As she held open the flap for the others, she yawned.

"Uh-oh!" Kara teased. "Are you going to be the first one to fall asleep, Em?"

"You can't be sleepy yet!" Taylor said. "We haven't told spooky stories yet. Or played Truth or Dare. Or even had dessert!"

"Dessert?" Kara licked her lips. "Hmm, that's true. What's for dessert, Em?"

"Ice cream," Emily said, suddenly looking much more awake. "I almost forgot! Daddy bought us a whole gallon of chocolate chip."

Kara was already heading back out of the tent. "So what are we waiting for?"

Twenty minutes later the girls were back in the tent eating their ice cream by the light of the lanterns. When they finished, Taylor suggested playing a game of Truth or Dare. The others agreed, even though Kara was starting to yawn too.

But after a few minutes Taylor noticed something. "Hey!" she said. "You guys are all choosing truth!"

Jo yawned. "I can't help it," she said. "It's easier to answer a truth question. I'm too tired to do any of your crazy dares, Taylor."

"Me too," Emily admitted.

"Me three!" Kara added.

Taylor frowned. All of her friends were lying down on their sleeping bags. If she didn't do something, she was pretty sure it wouldn't be long before all three of them were nodding off to sleep. . . .

✳ 8 ✳

Spooky Stories and
Scary Dreams

"Okay!" Taylor called out, sitting up so suddenly that her foot banged into her ice-cream bowl. She grabbed the bowl and set it beside her pillow for safe-keeping. "Enough Truth or Dare. It's time for spooky stories!"

Emily yawned so widely that her eyes squinched shut. "I don't know if I can think of any right now," she mumbled sleepily. Since she read so many books, Emily was usually the one to start off the storytelling.

"Don't worry, I'll start," Taylor offered. She knew that if she could come up with a really good story, Emily and Kara would be too nervous to fall asleep. Jo was a lot harder to scare, but so far she looked the most awake anyway.

"Go ahead," Jo said. She was lying on her stomach with her head resting on her arms. "We could use a good bedtime story."

Taylor thought for a second. She wanted to make sure her story was *really* scary. Before she started talking, she leaned over and turned down the lanterns. She didn't make it too dark, though. For one thing, that might make her friends even sleepier. For another thing, it might make the spiders think it was safe to come out and start crawling on them.

"This is the tale of a girl named . . . uh, Susie," Taylor began. She made her voice sound as spooky as she could. "One day Susie was going for a walk in the woods when she heard a mysterious sound from just ahead. . . ."

She kept going, making up the story as she went along. Lowering her voice to a raspy whisper, she explained how Susie followed the mysterious sounds until she came to a haunted graveyard. There, she was chased by a gang of terrifying ghosts. They swooped after her as she ran away as fast as she could through the dark forest.

Her friends listened silently for a while. Emily's eyes opened a little wider. She started to look more scared and less sleepy. Kara sat up and hugged her knees to her chest as she listened. Jo didn't look very scared yet, but she was listening too.

". . . and Susie kept running and running, dreading the feeling of ghostly fingers on the back of her neck," Taylor intoned eerily.

Emily shuddered and touched the back of her own neck. Kara glanced nervously into the corners of the tent. Taylor smiled. They both looked pretty scared.

"And then something horrible happened," she went on. "Susie was so busy looking over her shoulder to see how close the ghosts were getting that she didn't pay attention to where she was running. She tripped over a tree root and fell right into a big hole in the ground! At first she was afraid the ghosts would be able to catch her there. But then she realized something even more horrible. . . ." Taylor paused for effect.

"What?" Kara asked breathlessly.

"The hole was very dark," Taylor said. "So dark that she couldn't see anything. But then she heard something—a terrible growl! When the moon came out from behind the clouds, Susie realized she was trapped in a hole with a—um . . ." She paused again, trying to think of something really scary. "A—a horrible, oozing, one-eyed giant squid!"

"Wait a minute," Jo said in her most logical tone. "Squids don't growl. Besides, squids live underwater. How would a giant squid survive in some hole out in the forest? That doesn't make sense."

Taylor frowned. Maybe she should have stuck with a bear or a zombie. "It's *my* story," she said. "I get to decide what makes sense."

Kara giggled. "Maybe it's really a zombie squid. Those can probably live on land. Anyway, that's a pretty good story, Taylor. Much better than the ones my brothers tell when they're trying to scare me."

"I'm not finished yet!" Taylor said. "Anyway, the squid reached out its tentacles . . ."

But it was no use. Kara kept making silly comments about the zombie squid and making fun of the rest of the story, too. Taylor guessed that was what she did when her brothers tried to scare her. And when Kara wasn't joking around, Jo was pointing out all the ways the story couldn't really happen. Before long even Emily didn't look scared anymore.

Taylor did her best to ignore them and keep going. But she noticed that her friends were starting to look sleepy again. She was starting to feel pretty sleepy herself. After a while she couldn't think of anything else to add to her story. There was a moment of silence that stretched on and on. Finally, the silence was broken by the sound of Kara snoring softly.

Maybe I was worried about nothing, Taylor told herself drowsily. She leaned back and rested her head on her pillow. *After all, I haven't even seen a spider since we've been out here. . . .*

The thought drifted off into the night air, and she was asleep.

Taylor wasn't sure how long she had been asleep. But suddenly, she felt herself come sharply awake. She knew right away that she was in the tent. But what had woken her?

A second later she felt something touch her face. Something soft and light, like tiny, hairy legs brushing against her forehead.

"AAAAAAAAAH!" she screamed at the top of her lungs.

✴ 9 ✴

Taylor Tells the Truth

"What is it?" Emily cried out, sounding terrified.

There was a moment of commotion as the others woke up. Taylor opened her eyes and sat up quickly, brushing at her own face. The lanterns were still on, and Taylor saw Mi-Mo darting out of the tent with his long, fuzzy tail whipping behind him.

She looked down. Her ice-cream bowl was still beside her pillow where she'd left it, but now the spoon was on the ground.

Feeling foolish, Taylor realized what had happened. That hadn't been a giant spider running its hairy legs over her face. It had been Mi-Mo's tail or whiskers brushing against her as he licked the leftover ice cream out of the bowl.

"Hey, what's the big idea, Taylor?" Kara sounded annoyed. She rubbed the sleep out of her eyes and glared at Taylor. Her red hair was sticking up in tufts on her head. "So we didn't think your story was that scary—that doesn't mean you have to try to scare us like that."

Taylor blinked in surprise. Then she realized that her friends thought she'd screamed on purpose to frighten them.

"But—but I didn't—," she stammered.

"It's okay, Kara," Emily said quickly, trying to smooth things over. "Taylor was just being Taylor. It's no big deal."

"I'm sorry, guys." Taylor felt terrible. "I didn't mean to scare you. I swear."

"Fine." Kara still sounded grumpy. "Does that mean we can go back to sleep now?"

There was the sound of a window sliding open in the house. "Everything all right out there, girls?" Mr. McDougal called.

Emily leaned out the tent's entrance. "We're okay, Daddy," she called back. "Sorry about the noise."

Meanwhile, Jo was peering at Taylor's face. "Hold on," she said to Kara and

Emily. "Taylor looks really upset. What's wrong, T?"

Taylor hesitated for only a second. "Okay," she said. "I guess I should tell you guys the truth." She took a deep breath. "I—I thought a spider was touching me. That's why I screamed."

Kara looked confused. "Huh?" she said. "Is this the start of another story? A giant spider to go with the giant zombie squid?"

"Nothing like that." Taylor shook her head. "See, there's something you guys don't know about me. I—I'm sort of afraid of bugs. At least when they're touching me." She quickly explained her fear.

"Why didn't you tell us?" Kara cried when Taylor had finished.

Emily shook her head, looking amazed. "I can't believe fearless Taylor actually has a fear," she said.

"Yeah." Taylor looked down at her sleeping bag. She was glad she'd finally told her friends the truth. But she also felt embarrassed. "I guess I'm not so tough after all."

Jo scooted closer and put an arm around Taylor's shoulders. "Don't say that," she said. "You're still the toughest person I know."

"Yeah." Kara smiled at her. "And don't worry—we won't tell anyone else. You know you can trust us."

"I know. But that's okay," Taylor said. "My whole soccer team knows now." She told them what had happened at practice the day before.

Emily pushed back her sleeping bag. "I just wish you'd told us sooner," she said. "I never would have wanted to do this campout if I knew you didn't want to. Come on, let's go finish the sleepover inside. My parents won't mind."

"Good idea," Jo said, and Kara nodded.

Taylor thought about it. Sleeping

inside would be a lot easier. . . .

But then she shook her head. "Never surrender," she whispered.

"What did you say?" Kara asked.

Taylor smiled. "I said, we don't have to go inside," she said. "I survived this long out here, didn't I? If I can make it through the rest of the night, maybe I won't be so scared next time."

"Are you sure?" Emily asked, still looking worried.

"Positive," Taylor said firmly.

Her friends traded a glance. They all shrugged.

"Okay," Jo said. "But at least let us help you. We can rearrange our sleeping bags so yours is in the middle. That way, at least the spiders will crawl on us first."

"Ew!" Kara said with a shudder. But she got up and started moving her sleeping bag right along with Jo and Emily.

Taylor was touched. "Thanks, guys," she

said as she watched them circle her with their sleeping bags. "You're the best friends ever."

"We know," Emily said with a smile.

As Taylor drifted off to sleep again a few minutes later, she was feeling better than she'd felt in two days. Why hadn't she told her friends the truth sooner? She still had to face her fear. But this way, she got to do it with her friends on her side.

At least she would know better next time. Because with the whole Sleepover Squad protecting her, she was pretty sure nothing would wake her up before morning.

Slumber Party Project:
Camping Dos and Don'ts

Do check the weather. Make sure you pack the right type of pajamas for the season, plus anything else you might need, such as sunscreen or bug spray.

Do play games like Freeze Tag or Kick the Can before it gets dark. Go for a nature hike or play ball with the dog. Camping isn't just sleeping in a tent—it's all about having fun outdoors.

Do look up at the stars. See how many constellations you can spot!

Don't use perfume or anything else with a strong scent. Otherwise, you'll be even easier for the mosquitoes to find!

Don't sleep in the same clothes you wore all day.

Don't forget your flashlight. You can use it to make shadow puppets in the dark or to find your way to the restroom . . . or to play Flashlight Tag!